little Miss Stubborn

by Roger Hargreaves

PSS!
PRICE STERN SLOAN
An Imprint of Penguin Group (USA) Inc.

Little Miss Stubborn was, as you might imagine, extraordinarily stubborn.

Once she had her mind made up there was no unmaking it.

If she decided to go out, she went out.

Even when it was pouring rain!

One Sunday, when it wasn't raining,
she decided to take the bus
to Mr. Strong's house.

Why?

Because she had run out of eggs.

And, as everybody knows,
Mr. Strong always has lots of eggs.

As the bus arrived, Mr. Nosey walked by.

Being nosey, he couldn't help asking:

"Where are you going, Little Miss Stubborn?"

"To Mr. Strong's house," she said.

"But this bus doesn't go anywhere near there!"

But Little Miss Stubborn took the bus anyway.

And you won't be surprised to hear it didn't go anywhere near Mr. Strong's house.

It went to Coldland.

A country where it is so cold
that everybody has a cold all year round.

"What a charming place," she said, shivering
and trying to look as if she had really planned
on coming to Coldland in the first place.

Which of course, she hadn't.

As you know.

She ran along a path to keep warm.

"Achoo!" somebody sneezed all of a sudden.

It was Mr. Sneeze.

"If I were you," he warned. "I wouldn't
take . . . ACHOO! that path. It's icy! ACHOO!"

"I'll take it if I want to," snorted
Little Miss Stubborn.

And she followed the path.
But can you guess what happened?

WHOOOOOOSH!

She slipped on the ice!

"That was fun!" said Little Miss Stubborn.

But of course it wasn't.

She came to a fork in the path.

"I shall go this way," she said,
taking the right hand path.

"You're making a big mistake!" said a worm,
popping his head through the snow.
"This way isn't safe."

"Don't be silly!" cried Little Miss Stubborn
and started off down the path.

She should have listened to the worm!

Before she had gone very far

an avalanche of snowballs fell on top of her!

One of the snowballs rolled off the path
and rolled and rolled down a very steep hill.

And, inside it,
Little Miss Stubborn rolled and rolled
down the very steep hill as well.

The snowball rolled a very long way,
all the way into a different country
where it melted.

As luck would have it,
Little Miss Stubborn found herself
outside Mr. Strong's front door.

She was soaked to the skin.

"My goodness! You're wet through!"
said Mr. Strong.
"Quick, come in and dry yourself
before you catch a cold."

"I don't catch colds," said Little Miss Stubborn.
"Anyway, I've come for some eggs.
Out of my way!"

"That's no way to behave," said Mr. Strong.

"Rubbish," snorted Little Miss Stubborn.

Still wet through,
she marched into Mr. Strong's kitchen.

Without a please or a thank you,
she helped herself to a large bowl of eggs.

"You could at least ask," said Mr. Strong.

"ACHOO!" sneezed Little Miss Stubborn.

"I told you you'd catch a cold," said Mr. Strong.

"I don't catch colds." said Little Miss Stubborn,
and sneezed again, "ACHOO!"

She was so hungry by this time
that, there and then, she made herself
an enormous omelette.

It was gigantic.

It was so big that it won't even fit on the page!

Then she began to eat her enormous,
gigantic omelette.

And the more she ate, the more worried
Mr. Strong became:
"You'll make yourself ill," he said.

"Fiddlesticks," snorted Little Miss Stubborn,
and because she was who she was,
she finished that enormous gigantic omelette.

And there is not much more to add.

Other than now you know how
extraordinarily stubborn
Little Miss Stubborn is!

Stubborn to the very end . . .
the very end of this story.